FOREST OF FAITH

A Christmas Journey for JESUS

Sharing God's Love Near and Far

SUSAN JONES

Illustrated by LEE HOLLAND

Good Books®

New York, New York

"Beautiful!" Badger exclaims, as the forest friends step back to see the decorations.

"And here is the star, just in time," calls Little Skunk. "Sorry I'm late."

"Where were you?" asks Little Turtle.

"I was on an adventure!" says Little Skunk.

"Can we come on your next adventure?" asks Little Bunny eagerly.

Little Skunk whispers to Badger what really happened on his adventure. He has an idea that fills him with the Christmas spirit and warms Badger's heart, too.

"This year, we're taking a journey deep into the forest for a very special way to celebrate Jesus's birthday," announces Badger.

With assignments from Badger and Little Skunk, everyone runs home to prepare.

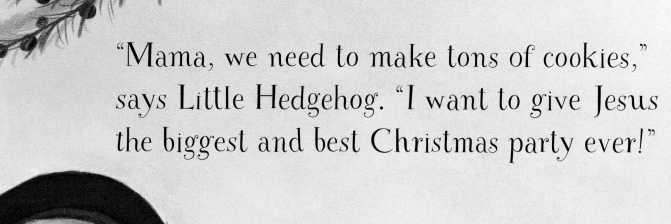

"Mama, we need to make tons of cookies,"
says Little Hedgehog. "I want to give Jesus
the biggest and best Christmas party ever!"

Meanwhile, Little Bunny and the Bird family are busy making festive decorations. Nearby, Grandma Turtle helps the little ones wrap.

"Let's plan for everyone to open lots of gifts!" says Little Turtle.

Soon, the forest friends help
Badger load the sled full.

"Make sure to get to bed early
to rest up for our journey!"

Early the next morning, before the sun even rises, Little Skunk rushes to the sled. "Merry Christmas, friends!"

Through sleepy eyes,
Little Bunny asks,
"Which way do we go?"

Little Skunk points and says,
"We follow that star to a
special celebration."

After at least a few "are we there yet?"s,
the sun comes up and the friends
round the final bend.

"Welcome to the celebration," says Little Skunk.

No sooner do the words come out of Little Skunk's mouth than the little animals run toward the sled, pushing to be the first to grab food and gifts.

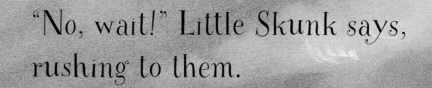

"No, wait!" Little Skunk says,
rushing to them.

"What's wrong?" asks Little Bunny.
"We're ready to celebrate."

As he looks up, he suddenly spots a little porcupine, beaver, and *frog* peeking out from their hiding place.

"Meet our special surprise: new
friends I met on my adventure
who would like to celebrate, too!"
Little Skunk says.

"Even better—a bigger party with more food, more decorations, and more gifts! What do they have to add?" asks Little Bunny.

"Absolutely nothing," answers Little Skunk.

"We worked so hard on the decorations! Didn't they make anything?" asks Little Turtle, confused. "Are you sure we even have enough food and gifts?"

"What we're sharing with them is all they have," Little Skunk explains. "Their families just made it safely away from a fire in another part of the forest."

"Jesus gave so much for us," says Badger.
"Sharing our blessings and caring for
new friends is our gift to Him."

"Our journey brought us to a very special place: closer to new friends and closer to Jesus," Little Skunk says.

"That's the best way to celebrate Christmas!"

Good Books books may be purchased in bulk at special discounts for
sales promotion, corporate gifts, fund-raising, or educational purposes.
Special editions can also be created to specifications.
For details, contact the Special Sales Department, Good Books,
307 West 36th Street, 11th Floor, New York, NY 10018 or info@skyhorsepublishing.com.

Good Books is an imprint of Skyhorse Publishing, Inc.®, a Delaware corporation.

Visit our website at www.goodbooks.com.

10 9 8 7 6 5 4 3 2 1

Library of Congress Cataloging-in-Publication Data is available on file.

Cover and interior illustration by Lee Holland

Print ISBN: 978-1-68099-628-9
Ebook ISBN: 978-1-68099-677-7

Printed in China